MAX MALONE, Superstar

★ Charlotte Herman

MAX MALONE,
Superstar

★ Illustrated by
Cat Bowman Smith

A Redfeather Book
Henry Holt and Company ★ New York

Text copyright © 1992 by Charlotte Herman
Illustrations copyright © 1992 by Catherine Smith
First edition
Published by Henry Holt and Company, Inc.,
115 West 18th Street, New York, New York 10011.
Published simultaneously in Canada by Fitzhenry & Whiteside Ltd.,
91 Granton Drive, Richmond Hill, Ontario L4B 2N5.

Library of Congress Cataloging-in-Publication Data
Herman, Charlotte.
    Max Malone, superstar / Charlotte Herman ;
illustrated by Cat Bowman Smith.
(A Redfeather Book)
Summary: After losing a part in an audition for a Peppy Peanut
Butter commercial, Max decides his true role in show business
is to manage the career of his friend Austin Healy.
    ISBN 0-8050-1375-X
    [1. Acting—Fiction.]   I. Smith, Cat Bowman, ill.   II. Title.
III. Series: Redfeather Books.
PZ7.H4313Mf   1992
·[Fic]—dc20   91-25191

Printed in the United States of America
on acid-free paper. ∞

10   9   8   7   6   5   4   3   2   1

KENNEDY

For Irv and Linda,
Susan, Andy, and Eddie—
and for my cousin Lois

Superstars, all!

Contents

Superstar

*M*ax Malone stood in front of the supermarket door. "Open Sesame!" he called to it as he took one step forward. The door opened by itself, and he walked in.

Max was heading toward the baseball cards when a bright yellow sign caught his attention:

> Hey, Kids!
> Star in a TV Commercial!
> If You Like Peppy Peanut Butter
> And You Are Between 5 & 10 Years Old
> Here's Your Chance to Audition.

When: August 15   10:00 A.M.
Where: Take-One Talent Studio

Bring a Current Photo!

The Peppy Peanut Butter Co.

"Wow!" shouted Max, running out the door and almost knocking over a customer. "I'm going to be on television!"

Max forgot about the baseball cards. All he could think about was starring in a commercial. It would be easy. Nothing to it. He had watched lots of commercials. And he loved peanut butter. Chunky style.

As he ran toward home, he pictured himself on the Silver Screen. Or was the Silver Screen in a movie theater? Well, it didn't matter. He could see himself taking a bite of a sandwich made with Peppy and smiling at the camera. He would say things like, "This peanut butter doesn't stick to the roof of my mouth." Or "It doesn't make me gag."

Maybe he would be smiling into the face of the

mother who wouldn't settle for any other peanut butter for her child. Or he would be eating lunch in school, and some kid would want to trade sandwiches with him. But Max would never trade a sandwich made with Peppy.

After he appeared on that commercial, other companies would want him. He would become the most famous commercial kid in TV history. It wouldn't end with commercials, either. From there he would get a part on a TV show. Maybe on one of the soaps. Or a sitcom.

By the time Max reached home, he was practically off to Hollywood. He couldn't wait to get inside and tell his mother and his sister, Rosalie, that he, Max Malone, was on his way to becoming a superstar.

Rosalie in the Picture

"I'm not sure if I want you running off to Hollywood," said Mrs. Malone. She was at her kitchen desk, filling out orders for personalized memo pads.

"You and Rosalie can come with me," said Max. "You can sell memo pads to the stars."

"All my friends are here," said Rosalie. "My whole life is here. How soon can we leave?"

"Maybe not for a while," said Max. "First I have to be in this commercial on Friday. Do we have any film left in the Polaroid?"

5

"What for?" asked Rosalie. She opened up a jar of Peppy Peanut Butter and took out a loaf of bread from the breadbox.

"The sign said to bring a current photo," Max answered.

"A Polaroid is not what they want," said Rosalie, spreading the peanut butter on a slice of bread. "They want a photo taken by a real photographer. A large close-up. It's called a head shot. I learned all about that in my after-school acting class."

"Well, that's not what they said," Max told her. He searched the desk drawer for the camera. At the same time, he wondered if Rosalie knew what she was talking about. Sometimes she did. Once when Max ordered a robot, Rosalie told him it would be a piece of junk. She was right. It fell apart in less than an hour.

Max found the camera and checked the little window for film. "There's one shot left," he said. "Let's go out and take my picture."

"Do you think I could pass for ten?" asked

Rosalie, taking a bite of bread. "I would love to star in a commercial."

"No way," said Max. Rosalie was eleven. But she looked more like twelve. And she acted like she was thirty-two.

Outside, Max posed in front of his house. Rosalie put her eye to the lens. "Okay, say Peppy."

"Peppy," said Max, forcing a smile. Rosalie snapped the picture.

"I can't wait for Friday," said Max as he watched the picture develop. "And I should tell Gordy and Austin about the commercial. They might want to audition too." Gordy was Max's best friend. Austin was Austin Healy from across the street. His father had named him after a car. Austin was only six years old, but an okay kid, anyway.

Rosalie snatched the picture from Max. "Are you crazy? Are you looking for extra competition?"

"But they're my friends," said Max.

"Use your head. Let's say the audition people decide to choose you. Except that they have just one more person to try out. And it's Austin. And everyone says, 'What a cute little boy! He would be just perfect for us.' Then it's curtains for you, Max Malone."

That Rosalie. She was such a know-it-all. But maybe this was one of the times she was right. Anyway, Gordy and Austin probably wouldn't even be interested. And probably they had seen the sign too. But if they had seen the sign, why hadn't they told Max about the audition? Well, phooey on them. He wasn't going to say anything either.

Max took the photo back from Rosalie. It was all developed. He had to admit it. He had come out pretty good. He looked like a kid who ate Peppy Peanut Butter.

"Now I'm all set for Friday," said Max, waving the picture at Rosalie.

"What do you mean, you're all set? This is just the beginning. You've got your work cut out for you in the next four days."

"Work? What work?"

"First of all, you need to watch lots of TV commercials. You have to study them and decide what's good and what's bad about each one. And you have to eat lots of peanut butter and practice auditioning. I'll help you. In fact, I'll be your coach. Every new actor should have one."

Earlier it had seemed so easy to try out for a commercial. But now with Rosalie, he wasn't so sure. Max looked at himself in the photo. He imagined Rosalie standing next to him, forcing him to watch TV and eat peanut butter.

With Rosalie in the picture, maybe becoming a superstar wouldn't be so easy after all.

Break a Leg

Max had two reasons for staying inside during the next few days. First of all, he wanted to avoid seeing Gordy and Austin. If he saw them, he might weaken and tell them about the audition. Or something might accidentally slip out. Either way, he'd never hear the end of it from Rosalie. Also, there was that matter of the extra competition.

Second, he had to stay inside so he could study commercials and eat peanut butter. He kept the TV on all day. At first he stayed glued to the set, watching both the programs and the commercials. But after the first day he grew dizzy. His head began to hurt, and his eyes began to blur. His mother told him that he reminded her of a zombie. So from then on he left the room during the programs and watched only the commercials.

He studied the way people smiled and laughed. And he tried to imitate them. He watched them being serious and sincere, as if they really meant what they said.

There was the mother who trusted the cough medicine she gave her daughter, because her doctor used it for his own children. And sure enough, as soon as the child swallowed the medicine, her cough was cured. She smiled up at her mother and said, "I'm all better." And you could believe her. Max didn't, though. He knew she was just acting.

He studied the way children gazed at their mothers with admiration when they removed stubborn stains from the laundry. And he practiced gazing at his own mother when she got the whole wash clean. He tried out expressions of excitement like the kids on the commercials had while they ate their oat bran. That took real acting. He knew that kids would never get excited about oat bran.

Watching the commercials was the easy part. Practicing for the audition, with Rosalie as a coach, was a different story.

"First we'll practice spreading the peanut butter," said Rosalie. "Now, do as I do. We'll each take a slice of bread and a knife and begin spreading." Rosalie dipped her knife into the jar and gently spread the peanut butter on her bread. Max took his knife and dug out a hunk of peanut butter. He also dug into the bread.

"Stop!" yelled Rosalie, waving her hands. Max gave such a jump that he dropped his knife on the kitchen table. "You're making holes in the bread. You'll never pass the audition if you do that. Try again."

After ruining four slices of bread, Max finally

spread the peanut butter in a way that Rosalie approved of.

"Good," she said. "Now, take a bite of it and say, 'This is good.'"

Max took a large bite and said, "Dih ih gu."

"No, no. You took too much. Watch me. You take a small bite the way I do. See?" And she took a dainty bite of bread, chewed, and swallowed. Then she said, "This is good," and smiled. "Okay, try again. And don't talk with your mouth full. And swallow before you speak."

Max was beginning to wish he had never told Rosalie about the audition. He wished she would leave him alone. Maybe he could do something to gross her out so much she would go away. He took another bite. Bigger than before. He chewed with his mouth wide open so she could see inside.

"That is completely disgusting," said Rosalie, making a face. "But I know what you're trying to do, Max Malone. And I'm not leaving until you get it right."

Max let out a deep sigh, finished chewing, and swallowed. Then he took a small bite, chewed, and swallowed and said, "This is good."

"Now smile," Rosalie ordered.

Max smiled.

"Oh, that's gross. You've got peanut butter all over your teeth."

"I can't help it," said Max, wiping off the peanut butter with his tongue.

For the next couple of days, Max practiced spreading, biting, chewing, swallowing, talking, and smiling. By Friday, he knew that he hated Peppy Peanut Butter. He hated peanut butter period! And on Friday, just as he was getting ready to leave for the audition, Rosalie stopped him at the door.

"Stop!" she yelled. "You can't go looking like that."

"Looking like what?" asked Max.

"You can't go to an audition dressed in shorts and a T-shirt."

"But it's hot out," said Max.

"It's also very unprofessional to dress that way. You have to wear a shirt and tie and a pair of long pants. Go back and change."

Max went to his room and changed into a shirt and tie and the pants from his good suit. He was already beginning to sweat.

Before she sent him off, Rosalie gave him some last-minute instructions. "Stand straight, walk straight, and smile. Speak clearly, and don't do anything to make them laugh at you."

"Why would they laugh at me?" asked Max.

"You never know. Maybe at something you do, or something you say. Maybe I should come with you."

"No way," said Max, shaking his head. That's all he needed. With Rosalie there, he could never do the audition. She would get him even more nervous than he already was.

"And don't forget your picture. It's not what they want, but it's better than nothing. And break a leg."

"Break a leg?" Max couldn't believe his ears.

Rosalie was always bossing him around, but she never wished for anything bad to happen to him. "What kind of thing is that for a sister to say?"

"It's just a show-biz expression. It means good luck. Only actors never say good luck. They say break a leg. I learned that in my acting class too."

"With my luck I probably will break a leg," said Max as he headed out the door.

While he was walking toward the acting studio, Max tried to remember everything that Rosalie had told him. He had to remember to chew with his mouth closed and to keep the peanut butter off his teeth. He had to remember to stand straight and to speak clearly, and to smile. The more he thought about all of this, the more nervous he became.

Max walked slowly. Very slowly. He wasn't going to rush. And if he got there late, so what? What was so great about being in a commercial anyway? Especially a peanut butter commercial. He was sick of the stuff. Why couldn't he be auditioning for something fun to eat, like pizza?

He reached the studio building a few minutes before ten and decided to take a walk around the block. He didn't want to get to the audition too early. At a few minutes after ten he went inside.

There was a sign posted on the wall that said PEPPY PEANUT BUTTER AUDITION. An arrow pointed up the stairs. Max climbed the stairs, following the sounds of voices coming from behind a closed door. When he reached the top of the stairs, he hesitated for a moment. Then he took a deep breath, turned the knob, and opened the door. The room was filled with people, mostly kids. They were sitting on chairs, as if they were waiting to see the doctor.

Two of those kids were Gordy and Austin Healy.

Competition

"What are you doing here?" asked Gordy.

"I was just about to ask you the same thing," said Max.

Boy, some friends they were. They knew all about the audition and didn't even tell him.

"I came over to tell you yesterday when I found out about the audition," said Austin. "But Rosalie said you were too busy to see me. She seemed too busy to see me too. She didn't even open the door."

"Oh," said Max.

"And after Austin came over to my house, I tried

to call you," said Gordy. "But Rosalie told me the same thing. And she practically hung up on me. What were you busy doing?"

Max swallowed hard. He wished he had never listened to Rosalie. "Oh, nothing much," he answered, and he sat down next to Gordy.

"You didn't sign in," said Austin. "You have to sign that sheet over there so they'll know you're waiting." He pointed to a desk across the room. Nobody was sitting there, but there was a small sign on the desk that read SIGN IN, PLEASE.

Max walked over and saw a sheet of paper with a long list of names written on it. He added his name to the bottom of the list. He had a long wait.

He sat back down and looked around the room. He noticed that Gordy and Austin were both wearing shorts and T-shirts. But most of the other boys there were wearing shirts and ties. Max wondered if they felt as uncomfortable as he did. Even with the air conditioning on he was sweating. He loosened his tie.

"How come you're all dressed up?" Austin asked.

Max shrugged. "I might be going away later."

Max saw that Austin and Gordy both had Polaroid pictures too. Nobody else did. They all had the head shots that Rosalie had talked about. Large, close-up photos. Max looked at his picture. His head was so small. And shadows darkened his face. He tucked the picture into his shirt pocket.

One mother was showing a man her daughter's head shot. "Little Patty is such a natural, don't you think? But then again, acting is second nature to her. I've been managing her career since she was three, when she starred in her first commercial."

Little Patty sat fidgeting in her chair.

"Loretta here has been doing commercials ever since she was a baby," said the man. Her first words were 'Roll 'em!' " He smiled at Loretta, who was staring off into space.

A girl about Max's age was having a mild disagreement with her mother.

"Now, Rita," the mother said. "Remember to answer when they talk to you."

"I always do."

"Don't just stand there looking blank."

"Mother, we've been through all this before. I'm a professional, you know."

Max was not a professional. He didn't have a head shot. He didn't have a manager. What was he doing here?

From behind a closed door, Max could hear a kid crying. And the next thing he knew, the door opened and out came a woman dragging a small boy by the arm. The boy was using his free hand to wipe tears from his face.

A tired-looking man came through the same door. He let out a deep sigh, and then he walked over to the desk to check the sign-in sheet. "Kevin Matthew!" he called out.

Next to Max, a boy about eight years old stood up. His mother turned him toward her and straightened his tie. "Now remember," she whispered. "Shake hands and smile. And act like you love Peppy."

"But I hate Peppy."

"Pretend. That's what being an actor is all about."

"But I don't want to be an actor."

"Of course you do," the mother said, patting him on his backside. "Now go on."

Max loosened his tie again.

One by one, names were called. Little Patty went in, and so did Loretta. Another girl of about ten was checking her face in a hand mirror while she waited. She wiped her teeth off with her tongue and smiled at herself.

Max shifted nervously in his seat. Gordy was biting his nails. The only one in the waiting room who seemed to be having any fun was Austin. He was smiling and humming and swinging his feet.

The waiting room emptied out as names were called and kids disappeared into the audition room. Some kids stayed there longer than others, but sooner or later they came out and left.

At last Gordy's name was called. He started slowly toward the door, where the tired man was waiting.

"Just be yourself," said Austin.

"And break a leg," said Max.

Gordy turned and shot Max an angry look.

"It's just an expression," said Max.

Five minutes later, Gordy was back out. He looked ready to cry.

"Boy, that was fast," said Max.

Gordy sat down quietly as Austin got up for his turn. Max told him to break a leg, too.

"What happened in there?" asked Max.

"There were three of them," said Gordy. "Only one spoke to me. The others just stared. They handed me a script. But I forgot how to read."

When Austin came out, he was all smiles.

"Boy, that was fun," he said.

"You were there for a long time," said Max.

"They wanted me to read the script twice. And they said we'll keep in touch."

"That's not what they told me," said Gordy. "All they said was thank you."

From everything Austin was saying, Max happily decided that Austin probably got the part. That there was no point in hanging around. And nothing could be better. Because Max had thought of a way for himself to be in show business without having to suffer through auditions.

"Okay, let's go," said Max, getting up from his chair. "Since Austin's probably doing the commercial, there's no reason for me to try out." Then he put his arm around Austin. "Come on, Austin, old pal. You just got yourself a manager."

Supercoach

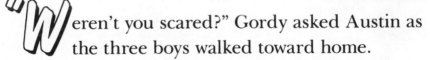

"Weren't you scared?" Gordy asked Austin as the three boys walked toward home.

"A little. When I first walked into the audition room. But I kept remembering my mother saying, 'Just be yourself.' Then everything went great."

"What does that mean—just be yourself?" asked Max.

"It means you should act natural," said Austin. "Don't try to be someone you're not."

Max thought this over. The whole time he was in

the waiting room, he hadn't felt like himself at all. He felt like he was someone else. Maybe he should have worn shorts and a T-shirt.

"I'll bet you anything you got the part," said Max, taking off his tie. "Now you'll need a manager. And a coach. All new actors should have them. And that's where I come in. The first thing we have to do is get you some good head shots. You can't use those little instant pictures anymore. We'll have to find you a photographer." Max was beginning to feel like himself again.

"I'll be the photographer," said Gordy. "My father's got a real good camera that he'll let me use. I would've used it for the audition today, but there was no time to get the picture developed."

"Boy, this is great," said Austin, smiling up at his friends. "When do we start?"

"Tomorrow," said Max. "Gordy, you bring the camera and we'll get started first thing."

Max needed to wait until tomorrow. Today he

had to deal with Rosalie. What would he say to her? What would she say to him?

"You what?" Rosalie screamed. "You left without auditioning?" She slapped her forehead and sank into a chair. "I can't believe you would do something so stupid."

"Like I told you," said Max, "Austin probably got the part. There was no reason for me to audition."

All the way home, Max had been thinking of the excuses he could give to Rosalie. He could say that he never got around to auditioning; that he fainted from the heat because of the shirt and tie she made him wear. Or he could say that he auditioned and now he had to wait for them to be in touch. But he didn't want to lie. And besides, Gordy and Austin knew that none of that had happened, and they might say something.

Or he could tell the truth. That he was too nervous to go through with the audition. But Rosalie would never understand that. It didn't look like she was understanding this, either.

"You don't know for sure that Austin got the part, do you?" Rosalie pushed on. "And even if they were thinking of him, maybe they would've liked you better. I can't believe you did that." She slapped her forehead again.

Max left Rosalie in the middle of her outburst and went to his room to change into shorts and a T-shirt. Then he went into the kitchen to get himself a drink of ice-cold water. He felt better already.

Mrs. Malone was at her desk, admiring an order that had just come in from the printer.

"New memo pads?" Max asked as he sat down at the kitchen table.

"No," said his mother. "Personalized address labels. I'm branching out." She got up from her desk and took a seat next to Max.

"Tough day, huh?"

Max took a sip of water and nodded. "I only thought about how easy it would be to do a commercial. I never even thought about how hard it would be to audition."

"I guess nothing is as easy as it seems," said his mother.

"For Austin it is."

"Maybe," said his mother.

After dinner, Max noticed that Rosalie sat glued to the TV set. Probably watching another old movie, he decided. Rosalie loved old movies. Especially love stories. Like *Gone With the Wind*.

"Watching an old movie?" Max asked her.

"No," said Rosalie. "Something almost as good. It's all about how women prepare for beauty pageants. Like Miss America. Or Miss Universe. Or Miss Laguna Beach. Some of them start when they're just babies."

Max sat down next to Rosalie and watched the screen. Little girls with makeup and grown-up hairdos were parading across a stage to music.

They wore evening gowns that looked like adult gowns that had shrunk in the wash.

"Look at those sappy smiles," said Max. "They look like they're plastered onto their faces."

"Shhh," said Rosalie. "I'm trying to listen."

"They look like miniature ladies," said Max.

"They start them young," said Rosalie. "One mother told how she carried her child across the stage when the little girl was just eight months old."

"An eight-month-old baby should be home playing with its toes," said Max.

As the show continued, Max saw how the contestants prepared for the pageants. They had to practice standing, walking, and turning. They had to practice holding a smile for a long time.

"Hold it just a little longer," the coach was saying. "Make that smile last. And try smiling with your eyes, too."

Max counted to himself to see how long he could hold a smile before it started to hurt. He practiced smiling with his eyes.

The contestants learned how to answer questions. "The way you answer can be more important than what you say," the coach told them. "Don't roll your eyes up to the ceiling. Don't hesitate with lots of 'uhs' and 'ums.' Think *winner.* Believe in yourself."

When they began working on makeup and hairstyles, Rosalie became entranced. Max became bored. He got up and left. But he was glad he had watched the program. He learned a lot. Now he felt like a real coach and manager. One day maybe he would even be on television, showing the audience how he prepared kids for TV commercials.

He might become the most famous commercial coach in history.

Say Cheese

"This is a quality camera," said Gordy when he came by in the morning. "My father says you've got to have a quality camera to take quality pictures."

Gordy showed Max all the quality features of the camera while they waited on the front steps for Austin to come over with money for film. Pretty soon they saw him running across the street and waving to them.

"Did you have any trouble getting the money?" Max asked.

"Not a bit," said Austin, handing the money to his manager. "My mother says it's nice of you guys to take such an interest in me."

Max felt a sudden sense of importance. He puffed out his chest and put his arm around Austin. "Come on. Let's get your career going."

They started out for the drugstore where there was a sale on film. On the way they passed the supermarket, and Max ran in to check the bulletin board.

"Nothing about auditions," he announced when he came out. "But I'll look again tomorrow or the next day. Did you hear anything from Take-One?"

"Not yet," said Austin. "They're probably still deciding."

At the drugstore, the three boys stood in front of the film rack, trying to figure out what to buy. There were so many different kinds of film. Each row of film had boxes with different names and numbers on them. Numbers like *100, 400,* or *1000.* Or numbers with words like *12 exp., 24 exp.,* or *36 exp.* How did anyone know what to get?

The only thing Max knew for sure was that he wanted color film. The people at the audition had black-and-white pictures. But Max knew that color was better.

Finally, a salesperson came over to help. Her first question was, "Do you want prints or slides?"

Max thought for a moment. "Prints, I guess." He didn't know what "prints" were, but he knew he didn't want slides.

"And how many exposures did you want?"

"Exposures?" Max asked. He looked to Gordy and Austin for help. But they just shrugged.

"How many pictures do you want to take? Twelve, twenty-four, or thirty-six?"

"Thirty-six," Max said right away. The more the better.

"And what speed of film?" she asked. This time all three boys shrugged. Max had never realized how complicated it was to buy film.

"Well, do you plan to shoot indoors or outdoors?"

"Indoors," said Gordy. "It's too hot to take them outside."

"Will you be using flash or available light?"

This time Max just let Gordy answer. After all, he was the photographer.

"Flash," said Gordy.

They ended up buying a roll of 100-speed film for prints, 36 exp.

Back at Max's house, Gordy loaded the film into the camera and set up the flash. Then he and Max posed Austin in front of the living-room draperies.

"Okay now," said Gordy. "When I count to three, say cheese. One, two, three."

"Cheese," said Austin, smiling and showing his missing teeth.

"Good shot," said Gordy. "Now we'll take another one. Closer, this time. One, two, three."

"Cheese pizza," said Austin.

"With pepperoni," Max added.

"And anchovies," said Gordy, and all three boys laughed together.

"Get even closer for the next one," Max advised. "We want a real head shot."

Gordy moved in closer. "Ready now. One, two, three."

"Cream cheese," said Austin.

"With pickles," said Gordy.

"And onions," said Max.

"And liver," said Austin.

"Yuck," they all said. And they began holding their stomachs and making gagging sounds.

After they recovered, Gordy took more pictures of Austin in front of the draperies. Then they moved him in front of a plain white wall.

"Keep 'em close," Max kept reminding Gordy. "We'll pick the best picture and enlarge it."

"We still have twenty-six shots left," said Gordy after he had taken a few pictures. "What should we take now?"

"Ten pictures?" said Max. "That's all we took?"

42 ☆ MAX MALONE, SUPERSTAR

Max had never realized how long it would take to use up thirty-six pictures. Maybe they should have bought a roll of 24 exp. Or 12.

"Take some of me and Austin," said Max as he went over to stand next to Austin. Gordy snapped a few pictures and handed the camera to Austin.

"Now take some of me and Max."

After Austin took the pictures, he handed the camera to Max. "Now take some of me and Gordy."

Next Max called for Rosalie so she could take a picture of the three of them. Then Gordy took some pictures of Rosalie.

"Get real close," she said. "And take my good side." She turned slightly to the right. "Now take my other good side." She turned slightly to the left.

After that they took some pictures of Max's mother. And finally, all thirty-six pictures were used up. They went to the drugstore to bring in the film.

"This was a tough day," said Gordy as they were

walking back home. "But if we get quality pictures, it'll be worth the work."

"I think the hardest part is over," said Max. "Now that we've taken the pictures, we're ready to go."

"Go where?" asked Austin.

"I don't know yet," Max answered. "Maybe to do the Peppy commercial. Maybe to do another audition. But whatever it is, Austin, old pal, we're on our way."

Résumé

"I can't believe it!" said Max, throwing the newspaper onto the floor. "Little Patty got the part in the Peppy commercial."

He picked up the newspaper and looked at the article again to make sure he was seeing right.

"Who is Little Patty?" asked Mrs. Malone. She was getting boxes of memo pads ready for the UPS man to pick up and deliver for her.

"She's some kid I saw at the audition," said Max. "This is her picture right here. It's the same girl."

Mrs. Malone took the paper from Max and read parts of it out loud.

> ...She has a long list of commercials to her credit, having begun in television at the age of three.... She recently played the part of an orphan in her school's production of *Annie*....

"Lucky for her," said Mrs. Malone.

"Unlucky for Austin," said Max. He picked up the phone and dialed Austin's number. Austin answered.

"Austin, it's me, Max. I don't know how to tell you this, but . . ."

"I didn't get the part," said Austin. "I know. I read it in the paper."

"I'll find you another audition, Austin. Don't worry about it. We'll keep in touch." Max hung up the phone and thought about his next move.

Earlier that day he had checked the supermarket bulletin board for audition notices. When he couldn't find anything, he bought a newspaper to check that too. There was nothing about auditions in the paper either. The only thing he found was the news that Little Patty got the part.

Suddenly an idea hit him. Why not go right to the source? He checked the phone book for the number of Take-One Talent Studio. He wrote it down on his pad of paper that said *From the desk of Max Malone* and dialed the number.

"Take-One," a woman's voice answered.

Max lowered his voice to make himself sound professional.

"Hi, my name is Max Malone. I'm calling on behalf of my client, Austin Healy. Are there any auditions coming up?"

"Why, yes, there is, as a matter of fact," said the voice. "On Friday we're holding auditions for Zap toothpaste. We're looking for kids between six and twelve years of age."

"Boy, that's great," said Max, forgetting to speak in his professional voice. He lowered his voice again. "My client is six."

"Perfect," said the voice. "Get him here by ten A.M. and bring a black-and-white photo and a résumé."

"Black and white?"

"Yes. A black-and-white photo, and a résumé if you have one."

"Oh, sure. I have one of those. Thank you.

"Rosalie!" Max hollered. "What's a résumé?"

Rosalie came into the kitchen holding a hand mirror. She had been experimenting with eye shadow. She looked like a raccoon.

"A résumé is a sheet of paper that lists the actor's experience. And his hobbies and interests. And it gives a brief description of the person. Why?" She held up the mirror to admire her eyes.

"Austin's doing a Zap toothpaste audition at Take-One and I need a résumé for him."

Rosalie lost interest in her eyes. "Oh, really? When's the audition?"

"On Friday. And why would I need a black-and-white photo? What's wrong with color?"

Rosalie placed the mirror in front of her face again and began smudging her eye shadow. "Let's say they want to put Austin's picture in the paper. It's easier to copy a black-and-white picture than a color one."

Max was angry. He and Gordy had spent a whole day taking color pictures of Austin. For nothing. "Why didn't you tell me I needed black and white when we took the pictures?"

"I didn't know you were taking head shots," said Rosalie. "I thought you were just taking pictures for fun."

Max buried his head in his hands. Even being a manager wasn't as easy as it had seemed. "What do I do about a black-and-white picture? How can we go through another whole day of picture taking?"

"Just go in with what you have," Rosalie advised. "There's nothing else you can do. Anyway, if they like Austin, they'll use him. They can always take pictures of him later."

Max breathed easier. He wasn't going to worry

about the picture. What he needed to do now was write up a résumé. He called up Austin and told him to come right over. While he was waiting, he stuck a sheet of paper in his mother's typewriter and began.

Rezumay
Austin Healy

By the time he got that part typed in, Austin was standing next to him.

"Okay, Austin. First we'll work on your description. Let's go see how much you weigh."

"I weigh forty-five pounds without my shoes," he said as they went into the bathroom. He took off his sneakers and stepped on the scale. The needle pointed to forty-five.

"Now for your height. Stand up against the wall." Max took a ruler and began measuring up from Austin's feet.

"I'm three feet, three inches tall," said Austin.

"How do you know all this?" asked Max when he had reached the top of Austin's head and saw that Austin was three rulers and three inches high.

"I was at the doctor the other day."

Max went back to the typewriter and typed in as much description of Austin as he could think of. "Now for experience," he said. "We'll put in about the audition. What else have you done? Were you ever in a school play or anything?"

"I was Peter Rabbit back in kindergarten," said Austin.

"That's good," said Max. "We'll put that in too.

"Next we'll do hobbies and interests," he said after he had finished the part about Austin's experience. "I'll write that you collect baseball cards."

Max knew about Austin's baseball-card collection. He used to trade with Austin all the time. Max knew a lot about baseball cards, and Austin didn't know anything. So it was always an easy trade for Max, but an unfair trade for Austin.

Max didn't like being unfair. So he had stopped trading with him.

"What else are you interested in?" Max asked.

"I'm interested in Newton," said Austin.

"Oh, yeah. Your pet newt. That's good too."

Max typed in all the information. When he was finished, he pulled the sheet out of the typewriter and handed it to Austin. "Well, here it is, Austin. Your résumé. What do you think?"

Rezumay
Austin Healy

Description
Height 3 feet 3 inches
Weight 45 pounds

Experience Took part in Peppy Peanut Butter audition and starred as Peter in class production of Peter Rabbit

Hobbies and interests Collects baseball cards and interested in animals

Austin read through the résumé and beamed. "Boy, this looks great, Max. Now we're really ready to go. Except for one thing."

"What's that?" asked Max.

"You spelled résumé wrong."

Practice Makes Perfect

"A week?" cried Max. "It takes a whole week to get an enlargement? We need it by Friday."

"Sorry," said the woman behind the camera counter. "But it's already Monday. And this order won't go out until tomorrow."

"Let's forget it," said Gordy. "None of these pictures is worth enlarging anyway. We got too close."

Max knew that Gordy was right. Most of the pictures of Austin had come out blurry. There was a pretty good picture of him in front of the living-room draperies. It was the first one Gordy had taken. Before he moved in for the close-up shots. That was the one Max wanted to use for the enlargement.

"We'll just go in with what we have," said Max, as he, Gordy, and Austin walked out the door of the drugstore.

"It wasn't the camera's fault," said Gordy. "The pictures of the three of us came out good. And the pictures of your mother, too."

"The best ones are of Rosalie," said Austin.

"The pictures aren't that important," said Max. "It's the audition that counts. And we have three whole days to practice. That's plenty of time. Austin here is a fast learner."

Austin came early the next morning with his toothbrush and a tube of Zap toothpaste.

"I'm glad you brought the giant economy size," said Max. "We'll probably use lots of toothpaste."

They went into the bathroom and Max positioned Austin directly in front of the sink. "We'll practice brushing," said Max.

Austin wet his toothbrush, squeezed some toothpaste onto it, and began brushing. He brushed from side to side.

"I once heard that you're supposed to brush up and down," said Max.

Austin brushed up and down.

"But I don't know if that's the right way or not. Maybe do both."

Austin brushed up and down and from side to side. He had toothpaste foam all over his mouth. Gross, thought Max. He had a hard time looking at him. When he turned away, he saw Rosalie standing in the doorway, staring.

"Why, may I ask, is Austin brushing his teeth in our house?"

"I'm coaching him," said Max. "He's practicing for Zap toothpaste."

"He's foaming at the mouth," said Rosalie. "He looks like a mad dog."

Austin spit out the toothpaste and washed off his mouth and toothbrush.

"You're wasting your time," said Rosalie.

"How?" asked Max.

"Do you think for a moment that they're going to want Austin to brush his teeth in front of them? Did you ever see a commercial with a person actually brushing his teeth? You always see them before they brush or after they've finished. You see them squeezing the toothpaste. And showing off their bright teeth. And bragging about no cavities. You don't see toothpaste all over their mouths. Yuck." She turned around and walked away.

"Rosalie is right," said Max. "Let's start all over. We'll practice squeezing the tube."

Austin squeezed a small amount onto his brush.

"That's not enough," said Max.

"That's all I ever use," said Austin.

"On TV they always cover the whole brush with a

long row of toothpaste," Max informed him. "Start from the beginning."

Austin washed off his toothbrush, and this time he squeezed a long row of paste that covered the entire brush.

"Good," said Max. "Now hold the toothbrush up and smile. Show your teeth."

Austin held up the toothbrush, smiled, and showed his teeth.

"Hold that smile," said Max. "Make it last."

"It's starting to hurt," said Austin, still smiling.

"We'll have to work on that," said Max. "Let's practice interviewing you now."

Max and Austin sat down at the dining-room table.

"Remember," said Max, "how you answer can be more important than what you say. Don't roll your eyes up to the ceiling and say lots of 'uhs' and 'ums.' Okay—we'll pretend I'm the Zap guy who's interviewing you." Max sat up very straight and tried to imagine himself as the person in the toothpaste company in charge of interviewing. He lowered his voice.

"Well, young man, I see from this résumé that your name is Austin Healy. How did you get such an unusual name?" In his natural voice Max said, "Remember, no 'uhs' and 'ums.' "

"My last name is Healy," said Austin, "and—"

"Smile," Max interrupted.

Austin smiled and began again. "My last name is Healy, and my father's favorite car used to be an Austin Healy. He never could afford one. So when I was born, he named me Austin. Now I'm his Austin Healy."

"Very interesting," said Max the interviewer. "Tell me, Austin, why do you want to do a Zap commercial?"

"I think it would be fun," said Austin. "And—"

"Smile with your eyes," Max coached.

"And," Austin continued, "I love Zap toothpaste. It's my favorite. I use it all the time."

Max could see that Austin was trying to smile with his eyes. He also liked Austin's answer. Austin sure was a fast learner.

"That was a great answer," said Max. "Oh—I'm being myself again. Let's see. What else should I ask you?"

"I think I have to go home," said Austin.

"Okay," said Max. "We'll practice more tomorrow."

During the next two days, Max coached Austin in walking, standing, and turning. They worked on squeezing toothpaste. But mostly, they practiced having Austin run into the house saying things like, "I had a perfect checkup. No cavities."

"Keep smiling," Max kept reminding him.

"I've been smiling so much my mouth hurts," Austin kept answering.

On the day before the audition, when they were all finished practicing, Max congratulated Austin on a job well done.

"You're ready for tomorrow. I'll pick you up at fifteen minutes to ten. Be sure to wear a shirt and tie."

"But it's going to be hot out," Austin complained.

"So what?" said Max. "You're a professional now. And I don't want you to be nervous. I'll be with you every step of the way."

★9

Zap

*M*ax was up early Friday morning. He put on a shirt and tie so he would look professional too. Then he checked his appointment book. In the space where it said FRIDAY, 10:00 A.M., he had written *Austin—Zap commercial.*

Mrs. Malone had given him the book the night before. It was personalized. On the front it said *MAX MALONE'S Appointment Book.*

"Every manager should have one," she told him. And Max had written in it right away.

Now, at fifteen minutes before ten and armed

with the appointment book, photo, and résumé, Max was off to pick up Austin Healy.

"Don't worry," said Max on the way over. "*Think winner.* Believe in yourself."

"I don't feel like myself," said Austin, tugging at his tie.

The audition waiting room was filled with people. Just the way it had been the Friday before.

"Go on, Austin," said Max. "Have a seat. I'll sign in for you."

After Max added Austin's name to the list, they sat around, waiting with the other people. Some of them were familiar. Loretta was there, and so was Kevin Matthew, and the girl who told her mother she was a professional. The big difference this time was that Max didn't feel the least bit nervous. He felt great. He liked being Austin's manager.

He looked over at Austin, who sat quietly, with his head down.

"What's wrong, Austin?" he asked.

Austin just shrugged.

Something about the way Austin looked reminded Max about the way he had felt the week before. He remembered the feeling, and it wasn't good.

All Austin ever wanted was to be himself. And Max liked Austin that way. He didn't want him to be any different. So right then and there, Max made a decision. From now on, he wouldn't make him practice over and over again. He wouldn't make him smile until his mouth hurt. He wouldn't make him wear a shirt and tie. From now on, Austin would go to the auditions just the way he was.

Max edged closer to Austin. "Hey, Austin," he said. "You know what we should have done? We should have brought our toothbrushes and toothpaste along. We could sit right here in the waiting room and brush our teeth. And get foam all over our mouths."

"Yeah," said Austin, smiling. "And we could be mad dogs. And scare everybody out of the room. And I would get the part."

"Or we could tell the audition people that we hate Zap toothpaste because it makes us gag," said Max.

"Or gives us cavities," said Austin, laughing out loud now.

"Hey, Austin," said Max. "Let's take off these stupid ties. Whose dumb idea was it to wear them, anyway?"

"Some kid who lives across the street from me," said Austin. He took off his tie and stuffed it into his pants pocket.

Max did the same thing with his tie. Then he sat back and glanced at Austin. Austin was smiling and humming and swinging his feet. He was himself again.

Pretty soon a door opened, and a young woman walked out.

"I want to thank you all for coming," she said. "But we won't be doing any more auditions today. We've found our Zap star."

Next a man stepped out. Max was in shock to see who was with him. Austin burst out laughing.

"Rosalie," said the man, who had his arm around her, "we're so glad you decided to try out. You're a fresh, new face. You're perfect for Zap. We'll be in touch."

Rosalie shook hands with the audition people and hurried over to Max.

"Oh, Max! I can't believe it. This is the best thing that ever happened to me. It's my dream come true!"

Max slowly recovered. Then a smile crossed his face.

"Rosalie, how would you like a manager?"

Before Rosalie had a chance to answer, Max turned to Austin.

"Don't worry, Austin, old pal. I can manage you too. I've got plenty of room in my appointment book."

About the Author and Illustrator

Charlotte Herman has written many books for children, including *Max Malone and the Great Cereal Rip-off, Max Malone Makes a Million,* and *Millie Cooper, 3B.* She lives in Lincolnwood, Illinois.

Cat Bowman Smith is the illustrator of the first two Max Malone adventures, as well as a picture book, *Good Night, Feet,* by Constance Morgenstern. She lives with her family in Buffalo, New York.